⌐⌐⌐⌐⌐⌐⌐⌐⌐

A TRIUMPH FOR FLAVIUS

⌐⌐⌐⌐⌐⌐⌐⌐⌐

A TRIUMPH
FOR
FLAVIUS

⌐_⌐_⌐_⌐_⌐

BY CAROLINE DALE SNEDEKER
ILLUSTRATED BY CEDRIC ROGERS

⌐_⌐_⌐_⌐_⌐

⌐_⌐_⌐_⌐_⌐

LOTHROP, LEE & SHEPARD CO., INC.
NEW YORK

To
My Nephew
DAVID DALE BALDWIN

TABLE OF CONTENTS

FLAVIUS was the happiest boy in Rome. His father was coming home from the wars. There was no doubt about it. Ships with strong oarsmen had brought the word from Greece, chariots drawn by swift horses had carried the news inland, and now heralds with trumpets were crying the message through the streets of the city to the seven hills of Rome.

"Lucius Mummius is coming! He has conquered Greece, he has burnt and destroyed Corinth! He is returning with his mighty army! Romans! Make ready for Lucius Mummius!"

Flavius did not know Corinth, or that it had been a freedom-loving city. He did not understand what a cruel, destroying work was meant by conquering. But he knew that all Rome was proud of his father's victory—so Flavius, the son of Lucius Mummius, was proud, too.

[1]

Never had he been so excited. He ran from room to room shouting to everyone, "Father is coming!" He ran into the atrium and splashed both hands in the central pool. The water flew and sparkled in every direction.

The atrium was the most important room in the house, so naturally Mummius would be welcomed there. Mother herself was taking charge of the decorations. She had been coming in and out all morning, followed by slaves with arms full of flowers. Now the slaves were hurrying to get out fresh garments for everyone. Lucinda, Secunda and Theodora, the little sisters, were already bathed and dressed standing serenely by the pool. Mischievously, Flavius splashed his hands hard in the water that sparkled in the sunlight slanting through the open roof above it. The little sisters squealed and ran to avoid the shower, while their mother came instantly to reprove Flavius.

"It is all very well to be glad," she said. "But you—a Roman—ought to have some dignity. Look, you have splashed the water quite over to the shrine where the little gods stand. I am ashamed of you!"

But she, too, was excited. Her face was flushed. Beads of perspiration stood on her forehead. She was ordering the slaves this way and that. Some to set the banquet table. Some to go to the market to buy food. Some to deck the whole atrium with flowers.

A few hours later, Lucius Mummius and his immense

army arrived outside the walls of Rome. Here he waited while the Senate was meeting to vote whether he should have a Triumph. They decided a unanimous "yes."

So in the evening, Lucius Mummius with a great company, arrived at his house. Very tanned he was, from the Grecian sun, tired and hot from the journey, but so glad to see everyone that he embraced them all, and greeted the slaves who stood in a crowd in the atrium bowing before him. The house was full of people.

Mother's eyes beamed.

"Oh, Lucius, you have been gone so long!"

"It's good to be home," Father said, and drew himself up with great pride. "The Triumph will be in two days," he added.

Flavius knew what that meant.

There would be a procession through the streets of Rome ending on the Capitoline Hill. It would be in honor of his father, and he, Flavius, the only son, would march in it. Victorious generals were sometimes given such a Triumph. It was the crowning glory of those who received it.

With the army outside the walls were many, many captives. But Father had brought twelve, who were especially handsome, to the house with him.

"You can have as many more as you wish, Tertia," he said to his wife. She looked pleased, but did not reply.

[4]

Turning to Flavius, he touched the shoulder of a slender young man who had come with him.

"Flavius," he said, "here is my gift to you. Ariphron is the finest slave of the lot. A man offered me seven hundred sesterces for him right on the battle field. But I reserved him for my son. He is descended from kings."

The strangest look came over the slave's face, as Mummius pushed him forward. Flavius could not tell whether it was fear or hatred. But as the man knelt and bowed before him, Flavius saw that his back and shoulders were trembling.

As Ariphron rose, his eyes met Flavius' eyes, and the look seemed to pierce Flavius so that he was afraid. The eyes were blue like flame. Flavius had never seen really blue eyes before. But his hair was Ionian black.

"Ariphron is to be your pedagogue," Father was saying. "He will wait upon you in every way and take you to school. He will sleep in your room at night."

"Lucius," Tertia said in a low voice, "are you sure that it's safe?"

"You need not lower your voice, Tertia," Mummius answered. "The man knows nothing but Greek. I don't want Flavius to be afraid of a slave."

"But he looks so resentful—so hostile," said Mother.

Mummius smiled scornfully. "They all have that look at first—especially Greeks. They soon stop it when they see it does no good." He gave Ariphron a meaningful look.

Then Father went back to his army. He was not supposed to be in Rome until he entered for the Triumph procession.

Flavius did not know whether to be pleased or only frightened by this gift. When his mother showed Ariphron to Flavius' little room, he dropped down as if tired to death and stared into space. He had a great gash on his chest and his right arm showed another sword wound.

That night, Flavius could not sleep. He didn't remember that ever happening before. Ariphron lay on the floor on a rough blanket. Flavius could hear him turning and twisting. It did not occur to Flavius to be sorry for him.

It was all very well for Father to say his son must not be scared. Flavius *was* scared. The boys at school often told scare-stories of dreadful things the slaves did to their masters. And Flavius knew of one man who lived on the Esquiline Hill, who had been found dead in the morning, murdered by his slave. The slave, himself, disappeared. Some said he had drowned himself in the Tiber. But maybe he hadn't.

Suddenly he began to tingle with fright. There was

a step in the room. But it was only Mother coming in with her little silver lamp.

It was a long time before Flavius fell asleep.

The next day was so confused and filled with preparations for the Triumph that Flavius did not think of Ariphron. Of course there was no school that day.

Early the following morning, Flavius with his mother and his little sisters, and all the household slaves started out for the Triumph. They made their way to the Appian

Gate and there they met Mummius where he waited to "enter the city." He greeted each of them formally as was proper to do in public. But Flavius, who was to inherit his glory, he embraced.

Then the procession started.

First the senators, magnificent men clad in pure white togas. With them were the tribunes, the censor, and the consul—all the officials who governed Rome.

The trumpeters followed, their long, silver bell-shaped instruments lifted high, and glittering in the sun, then litters and carts of all sorts carrying the spoils and booty of war. Never again was anyone to see such a treasure of beautiful things as these that Mummius had stolen from Greece. There were vases, jewels, crowns, golden vessels from the temples, paintings, pictures of gods and men, statues. Now they would all be scattered carelessly in Rome.

The crowds broke into murmurs of admiration, and cheer followed cheer. As the applause increased, Mummius was remembering all the other treasures that had been thrown away—the statues in Corinth that his soldiers had broken, the pictures they had used for draught boards in the street. He began to wish he had not destroyed so much, or sold so much to the King of Pergamum. Rome would have paid him better.

As for Flavius, never had he seen such booty; he was

having a hard time keeping up with everything. He wished the procession would move more slowly. The most beautiful thing of all, he thought, was a chariot edged with ivory, with gilded pictures all over it, drawn by two prancing black horses.

But then he saw the pure white bulls for the sacrifice. Their horns were gilded. Nothing could be more beautiful than these, he thought, watching the priests who came

carrying long knives with which they were to kill the bulls.

Last of all came the conquered Greeks—their kings, their princes, and finally the great multitude of miserable men, women, and children in chains; pale, sorrowful, some of them too ill to walk, some walking in silent pride, some loudly weeping.

The crowd, gibing and laughing, took this as great fun, and Flavius laughed, too.

In back of them came the lictors with their staves, the Roman guards.

And now it was time for Mummius to put on his magnificent gold embroidered robe and his crown of laurel. He mounted the large round chariot with pictures sculptured upon it, and the horses pranced and pawed, impatient to be off. The charioteer took the reins and they started.

Now Flavius, himself, was to enter the procession; as the only son of the conqueror, he was to ride just behind the triumphal car. His mother kissed him and he sprang on his horse. Ariphron, as he had been ordered to do, stepped up to Flavius to walk beside him. Then Flavius was part of that great human stream that was pouring into the city toward the Capitoline Hill.

Flavius rode well and even gracefully. From the age of eight, he had had his own horse. He knew all about

horses and was proud of this one which he rode.

They moved along the Appian Way, and the farther they got, the denser were the crowds.

They were standing and cheering each part of the procession as it went by, and when the triumphal chariot came into view with Mummius in it, the crowd broke into a roar. Flavius could hear the great noise of the army which marched last in the procession.

"Io Triumphe—Io Triumphe," they were shouting. Indeed, the doors of all respectable houses would be guarded this night, for when a conquering army entered Rome, you could not tell what might happen.

Now they turned from the Via Appia, into the Via Sacra, and they entered the Forum.

How splendid it looked. All the temples open. Flowers

and garlands everywhere. Flavius did not know the world contained so many flowers. The air was filled with fragrance.

Just beyond the entrance archway, Flavius suddenly heard, "Hail Flavius, Oh Flavius, Hail!"

And there by the temple of Castor was his whole school, twenty boys in all. They were waiting to greet him. They swarmed out to get closer.

"Flavius, where did you get the slave?" shouted Cornelius Scipio, the oldest boy in the school.

"He's mine," said Flavius. "Father gave him to me."

"By Jupiter, you're lucky," said Scipio.

"What's his name?" asked Gaius, another boy.

"Ariphron. He's to be my pedagogue."

"By Jupiter, you're lucky," said Gaius.

[17]

For the first time Flavius forgot to be afraid of Ariphron, and began to be proud of him.

As he moved farther into the Forum near the rostra, he passed a group of Rome's most fashionable youths. They stared openly at Ariphron.

These young Romans were deep in the new craze for everything Greek. Ever since Aemilius Paulus had brought the Greek spoils to Rome twenty years ago, this fashion had been growing. The Romans were trying to imitate the Greeks—to speak Greek, to quote Greek poetry, to own Greek slaves and statues. Some day they would even want their gods to be like the Greek gods. Some day the fad would be carried so far it would overwhelm Rome.

"If you ask me," remarked one of the youths, "that Greek walking by young Flavius Mummius is the handsomest prize they've brought to Rome."

"He is mine," called out Flavius.

"Yours! By Pollux, he should belong to an older person."

"A mere boy," remarked one of them to a friend, "will never appreciate that beauty. Look how he moves—like a god."

They had come quite close now. One of them felt Ariphron's shoulder, testing him as he would a horse or dog.

Ariphron jerked away in anger and scorn.

[19]

"Leave my slave alone," Flavius called imperiously as he looked down at Ariphron walking so close beside the stirrup.

Yes, he surely was beautiful. He held his head proudly and moved — Flavius wondered how he moved so smoothly and weightlessly. He did not know it was because every muscle of Ariphron's body was perfect and strong. And as he walked, he kept looking straight ahead as if he did not notice anything near about him—but was seeing something far away.

"He's mine," thought Flavius, "and this horse is mine. I've got the best horse and the best slave in Rome. They are my treasures and no one shall take them from me."

Now the horse began to climb the Capitoline Hill. At the top was the most important temple of all Rome. The temple to Jupiter. The great altar stood in front of it.

And here the Romans carried out their usual barbaric custom. At the temple top, in the presence of their god, they took the kings and leaders of Greece aside into a building and killed them as if they were cattle.

Flavius was not at all upset. It was the custom. And to a Roman, customs were almost like religion. They could not be questioned.

After this, the bulls were slaughtered or sacrificed and laid upon the altar fire.

And then Lucius Mummius descended from his car,

entered the temple, took off his laurel wreath and laid it upon the lap of the statue, Jupiter Capitolinus. A deep silence fell upon the crowds on the hill and down below in the Forum, even out upon the Via Sacra.

The Triumph was completed.

IMMEDIATELY after the Triumph, Ariphron's wounds that had been healing grew red and angry and the poison spread to his whole body. When he walked, he no longer moved beautifully, but dragged along as though every step hurt him. When they brought him food, he turned his head away.

Flavius' mother attended the wounds and dressed them with healing herbs every day. For the domina in the house must almost be a physician.

"But he won't get well," said the old nurse, Mara, shaking her head. "That kind always dies. It's his heart that is broken."

"But I don't want him to die," Flavius pleaded. "He's mine, and I don't want him to die."

"All very well, little master. But your wishing can't help; it's death in the way," and old Mara pottered off, shaking her head like a bird of ill omen.

Every time his mother dressed the wounds, Flavius

stood by. He handed her the oil and wine and watched every herb she put in the poultice.

"Are you sure you've got the right ones?" he asked.

"Yes, dear," said his mother. "I hope Ariphron will get well. Your father would feel dreadful if you lost him."

Ariphron never thanked Domina Tertia for these ministrations. He merely let her do it while he stared into space with those strange blue eyes of his. Many times a day Flavius would go back into the room and stand by Ariphron, gazing at him.

"Do you feel better?" he would ask.

But though Ariphron would sometimes look at him, he never answered.

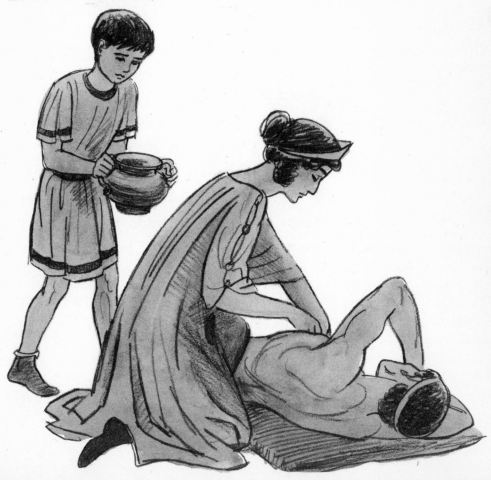

He was so weak now that he did not rise from his bed on the floor, but lay there all day.

Then one morning Domina Tertia was ill with a headache. She told old Mara to care for Ariphron. But when Mara came with the basin of hot water and the oil and herbs, Flavius pushed her away.

"You shan't do it," he said. "You think he's going to die and you'll put the evil eye on him." Flavius was afraid of the evil eye. He always wore a small chain around his neck with little half moons hung to it and other amulets to protect him. His mother, father, everybody believed in the evil eye.

"The foul furies take ye," said Mara angrily. "Saying such evil of your old nurse."

"I can put on the poultice," declared Flavius. "I've watched Mother every time."

"It's not the custom for a master to wait on a slave. Whoever heard of such a thing?" said Mara.

"I don't care. He's my pedagogue, isn't he?"

So Mara set down the basin in a huff and went away.

Flavius took off the bandages from Ariphron's chest and arm. When he saw the angry wounds, he clicked his tongue as he had heard his mother do. Then he washed the wounds even more gently than his mother had done. He was so afraid of hurting Ariphron. Next he put on the wine and then the oil and lastly the poultice. Oh,

[24]

very, very, carefully. He was so busy, so bent on his task that he did not notice how Ariphron was watching him, nor did he see the slow smile that came to his face. But when Flavius finished, Ariphron suddenly lifted himself and kissed him not on the hand as a slave should, but on the forehead. Flavius was astonished and delighted.

"Are you better?" he asked eagerly.

"Yes, child—better," answered Ariphron.

"Oh, I didn't know you could speak Latin. Father said you couldn't."

"I do many things your father knows not," said Ariphron.

Flavius was remembering once, when he was ill and the doctor wouldn't let him have any water, how parched

and dry his mouth felt. He hurried off, got his own cup and filled it with water at the fountain in the back garden.

Ariphron drank to the last drop.

Just then old Mara came in to clean up.

"And ye'll kill him now sure," she complained, "givin' water to a fever."

Flavius looked frightened.

But Ariphron spoke. "Never before have I heard that pure water was poison."

All that day with the persistence of a bird bringing food for its young, Flavius brought water to Ariphron. Water, water, water—until Ariphron could drink no more and said, "Have mercy, Flavius Mummius!"

And Mother, lying in her room, wondered who it could be who had sent that low musical laugh through the house.

Next morning when Domina Tertia came and took off the bandages, she was astonished at the improvement of the wounds.

"I did it," answered Flavius, much puffed up. "You'd better let me put on the poultice, Mother, for I am the only one who knows how."

Then Ariphron spoke to Tertia. "Your son, Domina, has a new remedy."

Tertia was startled, and a little frightened, realizing that Ariphron had understood everything they had said.

[27]

"I think he means the water," put in Flavius. "I gave him lots and lots."

"It was not the water," said Ariphron, and Tertia, watching him, suddenly realized how beautiful he was when that stony stare went out of his eyes.

Tertia could not imagine what Mummius would think of such a performance, but she was wise. She knew if she was to keep her son safe with this strange and vengeful slave, she must let Flavius do as he wished.

"Very well, my son," she said gently. "You shall dress the wounds. I will watch that you do everything properly."

THE HOUR OF THE DAY Flavius hated most was the one when he started for school. In the first place, Mara came and shook him awake in the middle of the night. Surely it was the "middle" for it was as dark as pitch. Then the slave came and dressed him. Except in summer, the hour was always cold. The slave's teeth would chatter as he worked, and Flavius would shiver in the dim light of little flickering lamps. It was no better when he was led out to the back garden to wash at the fountain. Then, breakfast in the atrium—always so hasty that he never got enough—and after that, a slave lighted the torch and they would go out into the silent streets.

But this morning, Flavius did not find it so bad. There had been a fortnight's vacation after the Triumph. Ariphron was now well and Flavius was to take him to school for the first time. He could picture the envious stares of the boys. All their pedagogues were old fellows tired of their jobs. No better than nurse maids were they, sitting outside the school gossiping all through the session. Well, his pedagogue was really a pedagogue—the kind of man a self-respecting boy ought to have. Hadn't those young men in the Forum said he was the best prize Father had brought home!

Flavius and Ariphron had breakfast together, and since it was so early, they fared alike. Bread sprinkled over with salt, olives and cheese. People generally had a weak wine, but Tertia considered goat's milk better for her son. A slave waited upon them, another slave brought the torch and books, the tablet and stylus, and gave them to Ariphron. Ariphron looked surprised and hesitated an instant before he took them. He had never carried a bundle before.

Together they went out into the darkness. The flame from the pine torch lit up the muddy street and the smoke trailed backward. All his life Flavius was to associate the smell of burning pine with those trips to school.

Flavius felt very important. Pedagogues led their charges by the hand through the streets. But since Ariphron knew nothing of Rome, Flavius was the leader.

The Mummius family lived with other aristocrats on the Palatine Hill. For this was before the time of the Emperors, whose palace—a square mile in extent—would sprawl over this hill and the surrounding valley.

The two picked their way down the steep street of steps to the Forum. It was necessary to cross one end of it to get into the Via Sacra where the school stood.

Here in the Forum, Flavius stopped. In the grey dawn the place was deserted save for a few public slaves step-

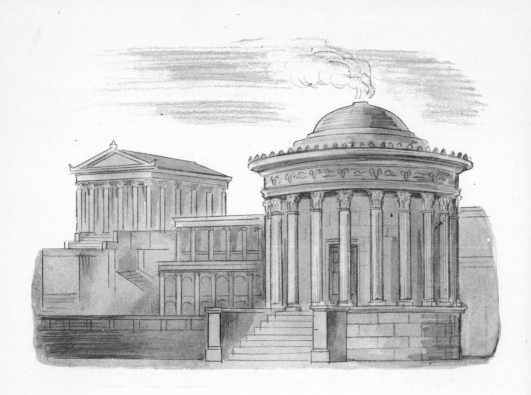

ping here and there on early errands. The temples stood
quiet and solemn as if they knew they housed the gods.
The round temple of Vesta was most sacred of all. From
the hole in the roof, the smoke rose straight in the quiet
air. The fire in this temple had been burning for centuries
and was never allowed to go out. It represented all the
hearth fires of Rome.

Flavius and Ariphron could look up the Forum to the
temple, and Ariphron pointed to the shields of Greece,
his conquered land, hanging along its architrave. They
could see the temple of Castor, the Temple of Janus—
with its doors open because there was still war some-

where—past the long colonades and shops to the Capitoline Hill. On top of the hill, dim in the early light stood the finest, biggest temple in Rome, which was called the Capitol. In after years, this forum with the many other forums, was to be the center of the world. It would be all of marble, with colonades and marble statues everywhere. But now it was built largely of wood and stucco, or of rude heavy stone.

Flavius stood there holding Ariphron's hand—looking up at him.

"Well?" said Ariphron with a whimsical question in his voice.

"This is the Roman Forum," announced Flavius.

"And what do you want me to say, little Flavius?"

"What can you say? It is the grandest spot in the world."

"That's well spoken, little Roman," said Ariphron, looking indulgently into Flavius' proud young face. "But for me, I must say something else."

"What else?"

"That I have seen far more beautiful places."

"You must not say that, Ariphron." Flavius' voice was half a command, half astonishment.

"I should not have said it, little Flavius, for to you it can have no meaning. Shall we go now to school?"

So they went onward and arrived with the other

scholars. And if Flavius expected to create a sensation, he was not disappointed. The boys stared at Ariphron. They whispered to one another. Scipio actually walked

clear around Ariphron, staring. Flavius was afraid Ariphron would get angry.

The school was an open portico built on the outside of

a public building. At this hour when the sun still had not yet risen, it was foggy and cold, but later it would be sunny. The boys sat in easy chairs; the teacher also. The pedagogues sat on the floor at the edge of the portico looking into the street. The teacher was a slave and received sixty sesterces a year, which was about three dollars.

"The twelve laws first," he commanded.

The boys began reciting by heart at the top of their voices. Such a din! The twelve laws had been given to Rome long ago and were as sacred as a Bible. On and on they droned. Then came arithmetic. Then reading in their native Latin. Then reading in Greek.

As this last began, Ariphron looked up with unconcealed scorn. He stood it for a while, then like a musician who cannot bear discord, he got up and walked down the street until he was out of hearing.

At eleven the school stopped. This was the hour for dinner and siesta. But the day was cool and all the boys went to a field east of Palatine Hill to play and exercise. Later this field was to have the great Amphitheatre Flavia for gladitorial games, but now it was just a field. The pedagogues went, too, to watch the boys.

First the boys ran races. Flavius was good in this and came out first several times—until Scipio joined them. But Flavius could not beat Scipio, for he was older and

his legs were longer. Then they started at the running jump.

At this Flavius was a real failure. He could attain no height in his jump, and he never landed right. Suddenly Ariphron was at his side.

"Look here, Flavius," he said. "That's no way to jump. You must stand so"—Ariphron stood in beautiful erect relaxation.

"Try it," he commanded. And Flavius, wondering, tried.

"That's better, but your face looks ugly when it is stiff," Ariphron went on. "Never let yourself get stiff. *Never think you can't do it.* Move your legs thus in your running."

Ariphron stepped back to the starting place. There, for a lovely moment, he stood as if measuring the dis-

tance, then he darted forward like a bird, like a bird, swooped up into the air and alighted as if he had no weight, nor need to touch the ground.

The boys were speechless with admiration. Then they

shouted their acclaim. Flavius ran to Ariphron and before he knew what he was doing he had thrown both arms around him, in a surge of delight and affectionate ownership.

"Will you teach me to do it? Will you teach me?" he pleaded. And the other boys crowded. "Will you teach me? Will you teach me?" they asked, shouting together.

It was all so friendly, so clean of the hatred and blood-shed of war, that suddenly the resentment and loneliness in which Ariphron had been living for weeks dropped away. He laughed. Flavius had heard him laugh like that only once before.

"Yes, yes. I'll teach you all. But it will take work and practice every day."

On the way home after school, Flavius said thought-fully, "I suppose you were a professional athlete."

Ariphron's face flushed with anger. "Indeed I was not. Every Greek does such things daily. He wouldn't con-sider himself a man if he didn't."

At home Mummius was awaiting his son in the atrium.

"Come," he said, "tell me what you learned today."

In awed obedience, Flavius recited the laws, making only a few mistakes; recited his oral arithmetic; and showed his tablet with its waxed surface on which he had written the Latin maxims with his sharp stylus.

"Does he do well at school?" Mummius asked Ari-phron.

"Your son has a bright mind and does well in his school," answered Ariphron.

"What is the drawback?" demanded Mummius. For he could tell by Ariphron's tone that something was far from satisfactory about the pupil or the school.

"It is the teacher," answered Ariphron. "He is no better than a hack. He will do very well for the Latin and arithmetic, but his Greek is atrocious. It is a waste of the child's time."

Now Mummius was not sure that he cared for his son to learn Greek. What was the use of any speech but Latin anyway? Yet it was the fashion. And since he, himself, was to have the surname Achaiaus in honor of his victory over Greece, Flavius had best know the Greek language.

"Do you speak a good Greek yourself?"

"I hope so." Ariphron restrained a smile.

"Then you are to teach Greek to my son."

In all this talk Ariphron had not once addressed Mummius as Master, yet he had so managed that Mummius did not notice.

Thus it was that Flavius each afternoon was dismissed early from the regular class, and Ariphron took him to a nearby portico and taught him correct Greek.

·IV·   ARIPHRON, THE TRAVELER

FOR WEEKS after the Triumph, Mummius, the General, was very busy with the army. He must disband certain troops, reorganize others, distribute the spoils among them, and keep them contented. More and more, these returning armies, made up largely of non-Romans, were a lawless element in Rome. For their general, however, they were a great power.

Mummius brought home so many slaves that Tertia had to beg him to take back some. The house was burdened with them. There were no duties for them, and they fell to quarreling.

Tertia was an economical domina, and never kept slaves for mere show, as so many matrons did. "Take them away, Lucius," she pleaded. "They are eating their heads off."

In all this while, Mummius found time, *made* time, to go home and see how Flavius was faring. He heard

[41]

his lessons after school; taught him the use of spear and sword. Roman fathers were usually close to their sons. But Mummius had been away on campaigns so often and so long that he scarcely knew his. As for Flavius, he regarded his father with enormous awe.

Mummius was a heavy-set man and had the proper manner for a commanding general. He never unbent and seldom smiled. It was not long before the men of the city began to talk of electing Mummius as Consul. This was the most important office in the whole Roman Republic. There were two consuls, who together, ruled with almost royal pomp. Twelve lictors or heralds walked before each of them when they appeared to clear their way.

Now, Mummius was busier than ever, with all the business of a candidate running for election. He seemed constantly to be talking with prominent citizens. For days at a time Flavius did not even see him, and lesson rehearsals were abandoned.

As time went on, Flavius turned more and more to Ariphron. In the first place, Ariphron made the Greek lessons an experience more exciting than Flavius had dreamed of. So each day he looked forward to the stories about Homer's heroes—and each day he found it easier to answer the questions in Greek.

At the noon hour of school, Ariphron taught the pupils, as he had promised, running, jumping, throwing the discus. The boys worked madly at these things, anxious to excel. They began to feel they were the luckiest school boys in Rome.

Flavius kept remembering that first morning in the Forum when Ariphron said, "I have seen more beautiful things."

At last he asked Ariphron. "If you have seen places more beautiful than our Forum, what are they? Where are they?"

Ariphron smiled dreamily, as if he were far away. "The Acropolis of Athens," he answered. "The divine temple on the height. Not so large as other temples, but of a perfection, a perfection!"

Then he began telling him about one thing after another built on that noble rock in Athens, until Flavius seemed to be seeing it himself.

Thus began the tales of Ariphron's travels. He had seen the great temple at Ephesus, the Pharos or lighthouse at Alexandria — that enormous tower with a fire burning atop of it which lighted ships far out to sea. It was the first of all lighthouses.

He had seen the pyramids of Egypt. "They are the oldest thing that man has made. No one knows their beginning," Ariphron said. "They are covered with polished stone ... and when the sun shines upon them, they dazzle the eyes. They seem like mountains for the gods to dwell on. But they are not beautiful. They are only stupendous."

"How did you see all these places," Flavius questioned. "How did you ever get to them?"

[44]

"My father had four ships," Ariphron told him. "I often sailed on them to see that the men did their duty. I know the ports of the world."

"Now tell me of Corinth," commanded Flavius.

"Corinth, Corinth," repeated Ariphron. And suddenly there came into his eyes that same blue fire that Flavius had seen on the first day.

"Never, son of Mummius," he said harshly. "Never will you know Corinth from me." And he walked away into the slave rooms. Flavius did not see him for the rest of that day.

Then Flavius remembered how almost always when Ariphron was alone and Flavius came upon him so, he had in his face a deep settled sadness. Flavius was too young to know it was despair.

One day Flavius came upon him sitting in the corner of their room.

"What's the matter?" he questioned.

Ariphron bowed his face upon his knees.

"What is the matter? little Flavius," he said brokenly. "Only the death of my father and mother, only the death of my brother and best friend, and the disappearance of all—all the rest. Only my city burning, burning forever in my mind."

After that, Flavius never brought up the subject again. Mummius had destroyed Corinth and it had been Ariphron's home.

ONE DAY while school was going on, a slave came
by in the street and suddenly stood still, gazing
at Ariphron who sat on the edge of the school portico.

"Ariphron!" he exclaimed.

"Epialtes!" cried Ariphron, leaping to his feet.

Flavius, in the midst of his recitation, saw and knew
at once it was an old friend who had met Ariphron.
Flavius watched out of the corner of his eye; saw them
talking together so fast, so eagerly! They were too far
for him to hear what they said, especially with the boys'
voices reciting all around him.

But after that, when the man had gone, Ariphron was
like a chained animal. He paced up and down. He exclaimed to himself. He turned around every minute to
see if the class was done. And at last as if he could stand
it no longer, he came up and drew Flavius away.

"He must go now," he said to the teacher, who seemed

a little surprised. "We have orders to be home early."

He led Flavius to another portico. There he pretended to start the Greek lesson, but stopped almost as soon as he had begun.

"Come," he said suddenly. "I have an important errand. Come."

He took Flavius' hand, and hurried along so fast that Flavius could hardly keep up with him. But not toward home. Flavius was astonished at that. Along the Via

Sacra, across the field where the boys practiced running
and jumping, out of that, into the straight highway that
led into the Porta Asinaria. Then off again into a nar-
row, twisting street where the houses got worse and
worse, and queer, desperate-looking people stood in the
doorways. The street became only a path leading over
rough ground into the valley beyond the Esquiline Hill.
It was the public dumping ground, all hummocks and
hollows, and it was also the slave burying ground, if
burying ground it could be called. For many slave bodies
were just thrown out among the old wheels, broken pots,
and dead dogs—and hardly sprinkled with dirt. The smell

was horrible. Here was one of the foulest quarters in all Rome.

"Where are you going?" demanded Flavius. "I don't want to be here!" But Ariphron did not even answer. He kept looking, looking. Sometimes he stopped as if he had lost his way. Then he found it again and hurried faster than ever. All this while he kept tight hold on Flavius' hand. Flavius began to be afraid. He was almost as much afraid of Ariphron as he had been that first night.

Far ahead, there was a low building. When Ariphron saw it, he exclaimed under his breath. He hurried yet faster. They came to the door of the building and walked into a room crowded with slaves who were working at tables.

Now Ariphron pushed his way among the slaves. He began to call, "Clymene, Clymene."

Then suddenly a young slave woman at the far end of the room gave a sharp cry and sprang up. Ariphron forgot Flavius entirely. He dropped the boy's hand, ran to the woman and took her in his arms. He pulled her through another door at that far end of the room, out into the open air. Flavius followed.

There he saw something he was never to forget.

Ariphron was holding the young woman close to him. He lifted her hand and kissed and kissed it. Then he kissed her forehead and her mouth. Sometimes he whis-

pered her name and she whispered something back. Both of them were weeping so that the tears streamed down their faces.

Suddenly the foreman of the slave house was out and upon them.

"What's this? What's this?" he shouted. "Back to work. Back to—"

Ariphron looked up with something between pride and pleading. "Have mercy. The gods have brought us together," he said. "Allow us just these few moments!"

The man seemed surprised. Ariphron kept the woman still in the protection of his arm. He spoke again without fear. "You will lose no work, foreman. I'll do all the work she leaves. Oh sir, are you not also an exile?"

The foreman had a cruel, hard face, but Ariphron had touched a soft spot in him somewhere.

He shrugged his shoulders and walked back into the Papyrus house without a word.

After this, Ariphron and the woman were very quiet. They stood there speechless and trembling, just looking at each other as if they could not believe that they were both alive. Suddenly as if out of a dream, Ariphron became aware of Flavius again. He held out his hand.

"Come," he said. And Flavius went to him respectfully, as if Ariphron were some honored friend of his father's. "Little Flavius," said Ariphron tenderly, "this is my wife. I thought she had been killed in the streets of Corinth. We had been married only a month when Corinth fell." Then turning once more to the young woman whom he still held close to him, he added, "I may tell you Clymene, that I would not be alive today if it were not for this boy."

Flavius looked so amazed at this that they both laughed, a strange shaken laughter.

"Oh, little Flavius," said Ariphron, "you will never know what you gave me."

Flavius was not quite sure what Ariphron meant. But something in his voice made his eyes fill with tears.

From that moment he loved Ariphron.

STRANGELY ENOUGH, on the way home it was that very word *love* which Ariphron used.

"Little Flavius," he said, "if you love me, tell nobody of what happened today."

"Oh, I wouldn't tell," said Flavius so seriously that Ariphron was satisfied.

The next day Ariphron gave Flavius his Greek lesson at the usual hour. But he shortened the lesson, then took Flavius by the hand and, as on the day before, began to hurry along the road and through the dumping ground in the Esquiline valley.

Clymene rose from her place the minute they came into the slave house. And Ariphron took both her hands and kissed her pale cheeks and pale mouth. The other slaves stared.

"We can't go outside this time," she whispered. "The foreman will not allow it. He is awfully cross today."

"Then I'm going to work with you," said Ariphron.

He sat down on the bench beside her and reached for the work. Flavius came close to watch them.

At one end of the long table was a jar of water, and in this stood the tall green stems of some plant or cane. The slave at that end was cutting them into the thinnest possible strips. Then these strips were passed on to the other slaves at the table, Clymene among the rest.

"I'll show you," said Clymene to Ariphron. She cut the strips across to exact length, laid them edge to edge on a tablet of wood, and spread glue over them. Then she laid other strips crosswise over them and pressed down with a flat piece of wood till there was no water nor glue left in them.

"Did you know that the papyrus you write upon was made this way?" Ariphron asked Flavius. "I've seen pa-pyrus grass growing in the Nile."

By this time Flavius believed that Ariphron had seen
everything in the world.

Ariphron tried putting the strips together. At first he
could not do it as perfectly as Clymene, and Clymene
kissed his hand on the table, pretending to scold him.

Presently Ariphron said anxiously, "Flavius ought not
to be in here. He might get some disease, or at least get
his tunic soiled so it would be noticed."

"You'd better take him outside," said Clymene.

And Flavius who was getting tired, was glad to go.

The dumping ground was certainly not a pleasant
place for a boy to play. They walked on until they came
to a clay bluff that looked cleaner than the other places.
And here they found what Flavius was to call one of his
treasures. Flavius saw it first. The edge of a wheel under
the overhanging bluff. It was an old chariot thrown out

to rot. In great excitement, Flavius began examining it.

"Ariphron," he exclaimed. "It is the very chariot with the gilded pictures that I saw in Father's Triumph."

"Yes," said Ariphron. "It's a Corinthian chariot certainly. I wonder what dear friend of mine drove it with his horses."

He fingered the rim lovingly. "The rim is of ivory. It's a wonder some jackal hasn't ripped it off."

"Jackal?" repeated Flavius.

"Human jackal," explained Ariphron. "See—the far wheel is broken. That's the reason it was thrown out. They'd rather waste it than mend it."

"They had so many," said Flavius.

"Yes, so many," Ariphron spoke with such bitterness that Flavius again realized he had said something wrong.

Ariphron went back to the slave house and Flavius mounted the chariot and sat there, pretending to be driving horses. He was completely happy. A real chariot and all his own.

But very soon Ariphron came back, bringing a boy with him. "This is Hiram," he said.

The two boys gazed at each other, round eyed, like all young boys unable to get acquainted.

"Look," said Ariphron helping them. "The wheel is broken. Do you think you could mend it, Hiram?"

"I could if I had a hammer and some bolts," said Hiram.

Ariphron went off and soon returned with a broken hammer and some rusty bolts.

Then the two boys fell to work. They needed a piece of wood for a spoke, so Hiram went out and found a piece on the dump. They worked faster and faster.

It seemed only a moment until Ariphron came for them.

"Hurry, hurry," he urged, his voice strained. "It is late afternoon. I forgot myself. Hurry, Flavius!"

AFTER THIS Ariphron changed so you would hardly have known he was the same man. He walked with a lighter step. He did everything more swiftly. And often as he was at work, Flavius would hear him humming a snatch of tune. Such a wild, rhythmic, stirring tune. Even Tertia noticed it.

"What is that strange melody, Ariphron?"

"It's a tune the oar master used to sing to the oarsmen

on my ship to make them keep time. I didn't know I was singing. I'm sorry, Domina."

"I like your song," Tertia said kindly. "It has the very splash of oars in it."

And whenever Ariphron and Flavius were alone together, Ariphron could talk of nothing but his wife. Flavius would much rather have heard of travels and shipwrecks, but the talk would always return to Clymene.

"I am not like most men," Ariphron said half to himself. "I didn't have just any sort of stupid wife a father might pick out. I saw Clymene myself. It was at a festival in honor of Juno, a procession. She was a little girl then, only twelve. But I could not get her out of my mind. I didn't rest till I learned her name. Then I'd pass her house. Great Hermes, there wasn't a window—not a single one. Flavius, be thankful you're not old enough to fall in love."

"Were you in love?" asked Flavius disgustedly.

"Was I indeed!" Ariphron laughed, showing a row of perfect teeth, and his eyes danced.

"My father had been oh so busy for my sake. He had a girl picked out, a nice dull girl as white as a cloth and rich as Midas. He showed her to me on the street. I said, 'what about Clymene, daughter of Dromos?'"

"She's too young. You'd have to wait too long," replied my father, thinking that delay would change my mind.

[61]

"'I needn't wait but a year,' I said, surprising him."

"She isn't rich."

"'But she's healthy. She belongs to a healthy family.' That won Father. Oh, but I was silly to be sly with him. He only wanted to please me. I know that, now that it is too late to tell him so."

"She doesn't look healthy to me," Flavius said. "She's pale as anything." And he was truthful, though uncomplimentary.

"Oh gods, that I could take her away!" exclaimed Ariphron. "That damp papyrus factory is killing her."

Even when not with Flavius, Ariphron sometimes talked of Clymene with another Corinthian slave whom they called Corinthus. Ariphron trusted him.

One evening when Flavius had gone to bed, and Tertia had stepped into the house next door to see her cousin, the two slaves talked in low tones for they thought Flavius was asleep.

"The foreman is cruel to her." This was Ariphron's voice. "I fear he will be more cruel."

"I'm glad my wife is dead," the other slave said flatly.

"Do you think Mummius would buy her?" came Ariphron's voice again.

"Never. The house is choked full of slaves."

"Might I ask Tertia?"

"The domina's the worst of all. She's a stingy one."

They were quiet. "That was a mean thing to say about Mother," thought Flavius.

"You'd best not let them know Clymene exists," went on Corinthus' voice. "They'll find out you go to see her. Then the fat will be in the fire. Mind what I say. You'd better stop going."

"I'd die first," said Ariphron.

"Hist, she's coming!"

And Flavius heard his mother's clear voice in the front corridor.

Tertia kept strict watch of her household. If a slave went out, she must know where he went and why, and exactly when he would return. In the evening and at night, Ariphron was supposed to be in Flavius' room. If he ever was absent then Flavius knew nothing of it. There was no chance in the day for Ariphron to see Clymene except that one hour when he was supposed to be teaching Greek.

Besides, now Flavius was as eager to go to the Esquiline valley as was Ariphron, or almost. He was fascinated with the chariot; he was fascinated with his new friend, Hiram, who was a Phoenician from Carthage.

His father had sailed as far as Ultima Thule in his ship to get tin, so Hiram said. That was the farthest

place in the whole world. Hiram himself had been as far as the Pillars of Hercules. "But that's not really far," said Hiram condescendingly.

"Why did you come away?" Flavius asked.

"They took me as a hostage before they burnt Carthage—the Romans did," said Hiram, his face suddenly full of fear.

Flavius had for the moment forgotten that the Romans had burnt Carthage the same year they burnt Corinth. He asked no more questions. But one day Hiram told him how Clymene had found him starving in the street and had saved his life.

"That's the reason I'm not a slave," said Hiram proudly. "When they throw you away, you're free. And that master threw me away. I belong to nobody but Clymene. When I grow up, I'm going to make money and buy Clymene so she won't be a slave either."

Such enterprise! Such adventure! None of the boys at school could boast of such things. Yes, Hiram was Flavius' best friend.

Today, Hiram was there before him, waiting.

"I've got a new game," he announced. "Let's play our horses can go over the water to Egypt."

"But they can't," objected Flavius. "That's silly."

"It is not. I've seen lots of pictures of horses harnessed to chariots and running and prancing on the sea."

"That was a god's horse—Neptune. We're not gods."

"Why not? You can be the charioteer and I'll be Neptune."

That settled it. For of course Flavius loved best to drive the steeds.

They mounted the chariot and their shouts sounded far out over the dumps and the refuse of the valley.

They played that they reached Egypt and they played war—driving their phantom steeds like the wind and sending the nations flying before them.

They played till they got tired out. Still Ariphron did not come. The sun began to sink low over the burying ground. The air grew damp and the smells got worse. Even the boys noticed it.

"Let's go find Ariphron," said Flavius.

·VIII·   THE TERRIBLE PUNISHMENT

THEY STARTED toward the papyrus house. But Ariphron met them half way. He was pale and more frightened than on any afternoon before.

"Hurry—come, let's run," he said.

But the ground was too rough for much running. When they got to the smoother field, Flavius panted, "What's the matter?"

"We're late."

"Why did you stay so late then?"

"Clymene couldn't finish her work. The foreman was going to punish her. I stayed till I finished it."

"Punish," repeated Flavius. "What would he do?"

"Don't ask me—don't ask me."

But Flavius knew. Whipping slaves for a slight mistake was customary; sometimes they were whipped until they died. And Ariphron knew it, too. By this time they had reached the foot of the Palatine. They toiled up the steep street and were soon at the front door of home.

There in the atrium stood Mummius. His face was like a thunder cloud. If the ground had cracked open with an earthquake, Flavius could not have been more scared.

"Come here, sirrah!" shouted Mummius. Ariphron, white as death, went to him.

"Where have you been?" he demanded.

Ariphron hesitated. But there was nothing to tell except the truth.

"I have been to see my wife."

"You have no wife. And well you know it."

"I have my wife," answered Ariphron steadily. "By the goodness of the gods, I have her."

"Well the gods are not going to be good to you now. I've been searching all Rome for you. I don't need to ask where you've been. I know. The school teacher has watched you. You have been to the lowest quarter of Rome. Day after day you have taken my son into that squalor and wickedness, letting him see and know what he ought never to see and know.

"Come with me! Out to the garden with you."

He pushed Ariphron in front of him, and they passed through the corridor to the triclinium and out the back door. The whip hung there in the garden.

It did not occur to Flavius to try to defend Ariphron.

[70]

What his father decreed was as the decrees of the gods themselves. Besides, Flavius was struck dumb all over, in body and in mind. Ariphron was going to be whipped. If his father whipped him, Ariphron would run away, and if they tried to capture him, Ariphron would fight till he died, or maybe he would already have jumped into the Tiber.

Flavius, whimpering like a frightened dog, crept into the triclinium. But he hardly knew he was doing it.

He heard Mummius say, "Stand there, rascal."

He heard him get the whip from its hook, saw him raise his arm for the first blow.

Like an arrow, Flavius shot out of the door and ran between his father and Ariphron. The whip fell and caught him straight across the eyes. But Flavius did not seem to feel it.

"Don't hurt Ariphron!" he screamed.

Mummius, dropped the whip, and at the sight of his son's bleeding face, he, who had gone through battle after battle without fear, was suddenly terrified.

"Tertia!" his agonized cry rang through the house—"Tertia, I have blinded my son."

He would have caught Flavius in his arms, but before

he did so, Ariphron had whirled about, picked up Flavius and fled to the fountain to hold the boy's face under the running water. For well he knew that running water was best for wounds.

As the water washed the place clear, he shouted, "He isn't blinded. It's his forehead."

And Mummius, at his elbow, reached out toward his son, but Flavius, now almost hysterical, repeated again and again, "Don't whip Ariphron! Don't whip Ariphron!"

"Silent—silent for the gods' love," said Mummius. "Could I strike anyone who has told me my son can see?"

Only then did Flavius cease to cry out and crumpled up in Ariphron's arms.

Now Tertia was there.

"Bring him to my room," she ordered. "Lay him on the bed. I'll get everything ready."

Lying there on the bed, Flavius began to feel pain, a great throbbing ache in his head. But he clenched his fists and did not cry. Of course he must not cry while his father was present. Tertia was bathing his forehead, first with cool water and then with a healing liquid.

Mummius stood at the foot of the bed.

"He is suffering," said Mummius, in a low voice, as if he were suffering himself.

"Yes," answered Tertia proudly. "But he does not cry."

Only Tertia knew how Mummius adored his only son.
But now Flavius became quite confused.

"Clymene," he began to mutter. "They're whipping her. They're whipping her. They're whipping Clymene."

"Who's Clymene," asked Mummius. "What in the world does he mean?"

"Clymene is my wife," said Ariphron. "I talk too much about her. I forgot he wasn't grown up."

Then he added, "He's so manly and like a man."

Flavius certainly did not look like a man there in the bed. He looked like a little boy who has been hurt. He kept tossing from side to side, saying "Clymene ... the whip ... Clymene. Where is she?"

After about an hour of this, Tertia said, "I wish Clymene were here. Maybe it would quiet him."

"Then she shall be here," spoke Mummius. "Ariphron, go fetch her."

Ariphron, his heart fairly jumping with a hope he dared not believe, started up.

"I wonder if the foreman will allow her to come."

"I'll go," said Mummius. Indeed he was glad of any excuse to do something, and to get away from the sight of Flavius tossing on the bed.

Two slaves brought torches. They were armed with swords, and Mummius had his sword. He knew that the Esquiline Valley was a dangerous place after nightfall.

So they went out, Ariphron directing the way, the torches flaring and smoking, to the burying ground.

"Ugh—it smells like a battle field," grunted Mummius.

They were at the Papyrus House.

Late though it was, a dim torch was burning and the slaves were just putting up the materials for the night.

Clymene saw them but was afraid to show any sign of recognition.

"Come at once." Mummius knew no one dare disobey him. "I'll send you back in the morning."

"Flavius has been hurt," Ariphron told her.

"Oh, not our little Flavius," cried Clymene in a voice that Mummius took note of.

Someone was following behind them as they left the slave house, but they did not know it. They hurried to

the house of Mummius. Tertia greeted them at the door.

"He's asleep," she whispered. She took Clymene's hand to lead her in, noticing how delicate and thin it was. She must be about fifteen years old, Tertia thought, but so frail, she seemed a child.

Flavius roused from his sleep when they entered his room and Clymene knelt by his bed. She took his hand.

"I am here, dear child," she said softly. "You see, I am all safe."

Flavius gave a little sigh and went to sleep again.

There was a small stir in the dim room, and a boy tiptoed in, scared as a wild deer, looking this way and that till he found and knelt beside Clymene.

"Who is it?" whispered Tertia.

"It's only Hiram," whispered Clymene. "He always has to follow where I am."

In the morning, Tertia said to her husband, "Lucius, I like that girl, Clymene. I believe she is all that Ariphron says she is. She's worth three of the ordinary slaves, and so gentle. I'd like to keep her close to me."

"Then you shall," spoke Mummius, whose wishes were always obeyed. "Ariphron, your wife will remain here."

EPILOGUE

As Mummius and Tertia grew older they depended more and more upon Ariphron and Clymene. One day Mummius announced that he had decided to make Ariphron the manager of all his estates, both the ones in Rome, and his farms in the country. Now, Ariphron and Clymene were treated as members of the Mummius family. Clymene felt like another daughter of Tertia's and no big brother was ever worshipped with more adoration than Flavius gave to Ariphron. And then, one day after a long talk with his son, Mummius decided that Ariphron and Clymene should be given back their freedom. Flavius

went immediately to find Ariphron. He wanted to be the first to tell him the good news.

The Freedom Ceremony was attended by many prominent Romans and was a solemn occasion that no one would ever forget. As he stood beside his father, his

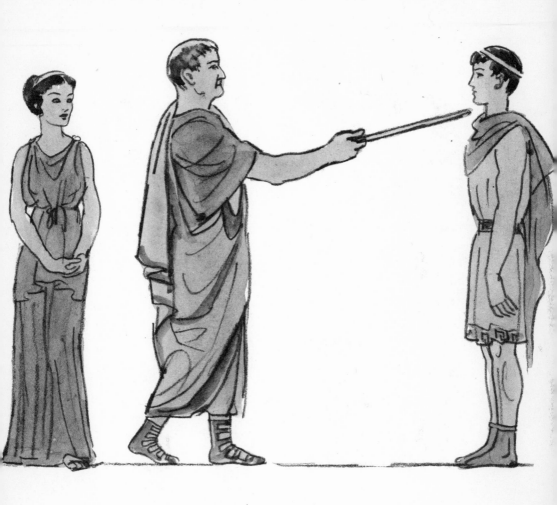

eyes shining, Flavius was thinking that this was the happiest day of his life. Happier even than the day he rode in the procession at his father's Triumph. For today they were celebrating an even happier triumph, and he, Flavius, had helped to bring it about.